THE *CURSED* STAGE

STONE ARCH BOOKS
a capstone imprint

SNOOPS, INC. IS PUBLISHED BY
STONE ARCH BOOKS, A CAPSTONE IMPRINT
1710 ROE CREST DRIVE
NORTH MANKATO, MINNESOTA 56003
WWW.MYCAPSTONE.COM

Library of Congress Cataloging-in-Publication Data
Names: Terrell, Brandon, 1978– author. | Epelbaum, Mariano, 1975– illustrator.
Title: The cursed stage / by Brandon Terrell ; illustrated by Mariano Epelbaum.
Description: North Mankato, Minnesota : Stone Arch Books, a Capstone imprint, [2017] |
Series: Snoops, Inc.
Identifiers: LCCN 2016033024 (print) | LCCN 2016035073 (ebook) |
ISBN 9781496543462 (library binding) | ISBN 9781496543509 (paperback) |
ISBN 9781496543622 (eBook PDF)
Subjects: LCSH: Children's plays—Juvenile fiction. | Haunted schools—Juvenile fiction. |
Twins—Juvenile fiction. | African American girls—Juvenile fiction. |
Hispanic American boys—Juvenile fiction. | Friendship—Juvenile fiction. |
Detective and mystery stories. | CYAC: Mystery and detective stories. |
Theater—Fiction. | Haunted places—Fiction. | Twins—Fiction. | African Americans—
Fiction. | Hispanic Americans—Fiction. | Friendship—Fiction. | GSAFD: Mystery fiction. |
LCGFT: Detective and mystery fiction.
Classification: LCC PZ7.T273 Cu 2017 (print) | LCC PZ7.T273 (ebook) |
DDC 813.6 [Fic]—dc23
LC record available at https://lccn.loc.gov/2016033024

BY BRANDON TERRELL

**ILLUSTRATED BY
MARIANO EPELBAUM**

EDITED BY: AARON SAUTTER
BOOK DESIGN BY: TED WILLIAMS
PRODUCTION BY: STEVE WALKER

ZIPPY 'ZA

PETS GALORE

HENSON PARK

DIAZ
GROCERIES

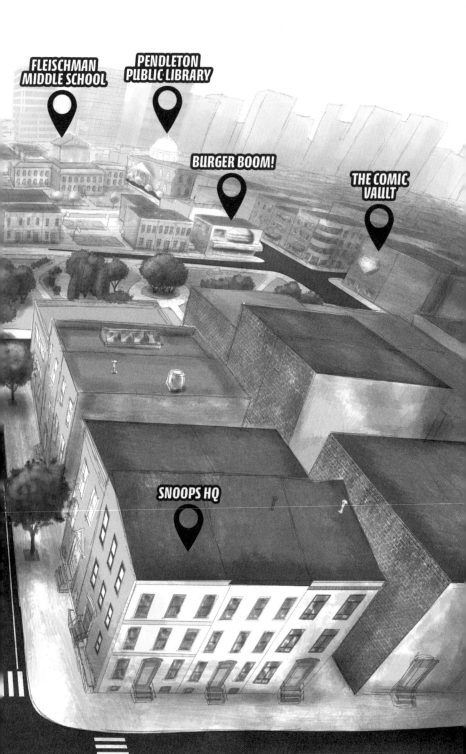

CHAPTER 1

A COMIC STAKEOUT

All was quiet in the darkened aisles of The Comic Vault. The store had been closed for over an hour. Its shelves of mint-condition, bagged comic books were draped in shadow. Its life-size cardboard cutouts of action heroes like Metal Miracle, Zom-Borg, and Arachno-Boy stood silhouetted in the store's large glass window.

And then the creaking sound of the door opening interrupted the quiet shop. A shadow slunk through the door and closed it silently behind him. Beeps and blips made music in the dark as the store's security system was deactivated.

"We've got movement." The whisper came from the cramped confines of the comic shop's janitor's closet, where twelve-year-old Hayden Williams stared at the tablet screen in front of her. The screen was split into four separate squares, which showed the video feed from the security cameras she'd set up in the shop.

The shadow, unaware of the cameras, moved through the aisle of back issues.

Next to Hayden, thirteen-year-old Keisha Turner leaned in. "Bingo," Keisha said, her excited eyes lit by the tablet's blue glow.

"Oh man, I love stakeouts," Hayden's twin brother, Jaden, said. He flipped closed the issue of *Ghost Pirates* he'd been reading and placed it atop the stack of comics beside him. A strip of red licorice hung limply from the corner of his mouth.

The trio huddled together and watched as the shadowy figure crept toward the store's glass counter, where all of the valuable comics were stored. A single comic lay next to the store's cash register.

"He's going right for the decoy," Jaden said excitedly.

"Our plan is working," Keisha said.

The team had been hired by The Comic Vault's owner, Burl Nicholson. The young detectives liked Burl. He was like a big teddy bear with a full, bushy beard. He let the gang hang out in his store for as long as they wanted.

Burl was suspicious that one of his employees, a skinny man named George, was stealing valuable comics and reselling them online. So Hayden had printed out a fake copy of *Action Man #1*. In mint condition, the issue was worth nearly $1,000. Earlier that day, Jaden had brought the comic into the store. He'd sold it to a nervous-looking George for just a few bucks.

"Looks like Burl was right about George," Jaden said as the shadowy figure snatched the fake comic off the counter.

"Time to shine a little light on the situation," Hayden said coyly. She tapped a button on her tablet just as Keisha shouldered open the closet door.

Brilliant light filled every corner of the store. Music blared through the speakers, playing the theme song from the Arachno-Boy cartoon.

George stood by the counter, a frozen statue of fright. His wide eyes looked terrified. His hands clutched the fake *Action Man* comic. Keisha dashed forward, past shelves of old plastic robots and giant lizard toys. Hayden and Jaden poured out of the closet after her.

"Stop right there!" Keisha yelled.

But George didn't stop. His instincts kicked in, and the skinny thief panicked and bolted for the store's front door. He wove down one aisle, past the statues and cardboard cutouts.

As he did, one of the cutouts — Action Man himself, his cape billowing — jumped out in front of him.

"Ahhhh!" George's high-pitched scream echoed through the empty comic book shop. He stumbled back and fell to the floor. The fake issue of *Action Man* slipped from his hand, landing next to him.

"Halt," Action Man said. "By the order of Action Man, protector of Cy-ton 5, defender of Earth!"

"Nice goin', Action Man," Jaden said as he, Hayden, and Keisha approached.

"Really getting into character, aren't you?" Keisha joked.

Action Man stepped out of the shadows. Only he was not an alien sent from a distant planet to protect Earth. The superhero standing before them was actually fourteen-year-old Carlos Diaz, leader of the squad of kid detectives.

Carlos smiled wide. "Hey, man," he said. "I always wanted to be a superhero."

George, still dazed and seated on the floor, looked up at the quartet. "Who . . . who are you?"

Carlos placed his hands on his hips triumphantly. "We're the protectors of local comic shops and defenders of the law," he said. "You've just been busted by Snoops, Incorporated."

Keisha shook her head. "Dude, that's cheesy. Even for *you*."

CHAPTER 2

THE PLAY'S THE THING

"Hurry!" Keisha said, looking over her shoulder at Carlos. "We're already gonna be late."

The following afternoon the two teens hurried through the halls of Fleischman Middle School. Draped in the seventh-grade girl's arms were a whole closet's worth of brightly colored coats and ruffled dresses.

"I'm moving as fast as I can," Carlos said, peering around the stack of shoe boxes and

hatboxes he was carrying. "What do we have to hurry for anyway?"

"I told Alyssa we'd bring these costumes to the auditorium before play practice started," she explained. Peering at the clock on the school's wall, she added, "Which was about five minutes ago."

"Okay, okay." Carlos shifted the weight of the teetering boxes as he quickened his pace. The eighth grader managed to keep up, but the boxes nearly tumbled to the floor.

Alyssa Wentworth was the stage manager for the school's drama club. She and Keisha had been friends since they were in kindergarten together, when they'd been the only two kids who could cross the playground's monkey bars without falling.

Keisha swung left as the hallway ended in a T. Ahead of her, she could now see the double-door entrance to the school's auditorium. A man in a blue coverall uniform and baseball cap stood near the door, hanging something on the wall.

"Hi, Mr. Ron," Keisha said. Mr. Ron, the school janitor, turned as Keisha and Carlos breezed up.

He had a thick gray mustache and piercing blue eyes. As he moved, the huge ring of keys on his belt jangled like a musical instrument.

"Why, hello," Mr. Ron said. He twirled a screwdriver in his hand.

"Can you get the door, please?" Keisha barreled forward.

"Oh sure," Mr. Ron said. He reached over and pulled on the metal bar of the nearest door. It yawned open, revealing a darkened auditorium.

"Thanks!" Keisha made her way into the auditorium, trying to be as quiet as possible. A spotlight blazed to life, casting its glow on the stage. Large, wooden flats painted to look like buildings in an old Western town lined the back of the stage.

As Keisha slunk in, a loud crashing sound rumbled behind her.

"Aw, man!" Carlos' frustrated shout filled the auditorium. Two kids on the stage, dressed as wild west lawmen and practicing their lines, looked up.

"Sorry," Keisha hissed, laying her armload of costumes across the back row of red auditorium seats and slipping back out into the hall.

Boxes lay scattered across the floor. Carlos was down on one knee, gathering them up. Mr. Ron helped. "I just . . . I didn't see your cart," Carlos said. A cart filled with cleaning supplies, a bucket, and a mop sat nearby. "I didn't mean to trip over it. I'm sorry."

"It's all right," Mr. Ron said.

As they picked up the boxes, Keisha's eyes wandered over to the display case on the wall. The glass case held a bunch of collectables from past performances by the drama club.

At least, it used to. What she saw staring back at her now wasn't old posters and trophies. It was her ex-best friend, Frankie Dixon.

"What the . . . ?!" Keisha blurted out. A poster for the upcoming play, *Wagons West!*, featured Frankie front and center. She looked like a Hollywood star. Her face beamed from the poster, with dazzling eyes and perfect, shining teeth.

"Is everything okay?" Mr. Ron added a shoe box to the growing stack in Carlos' hands and hurried over to Keisha's side.

"What happened to all the other stuff?" she asked, nodding at the display case.

"I was told to update it for the newest play," Mr. Ron explained. "Put all the old stuff in storage under the stage. I was just finishing up." He wielded his screwdriver and tightened the final screw on a sign below the case that read: Donated By Dixon Dental.

Frankie's dad, Keisha thought. *Of course he made them change the display to showcase his daughter. Ugh.*

Frankie and Keisha were once BFFs. That is, until The Fallout changed everything. Keisha hated even thinking about it. So instead, she grabbed a bulky hatbox off the floor.

Despite the loud crash, play practice had continued on. The two kids from earlier were now joined by a third actor. At center stage, taking up the spotlight like she owned it, was Frankie Dixon.

As much as Keisha hated to admit it, Frankie did look like she belonged on the stage. She held her chin high, her shoulder-length black hair pulled back, accenting her defined cheekbones. She radiated confidence.

The darkened auditorium was empty, except for one seat in the middle of the back row. In the faint light cast by the spots shining on Frankie, Keisha spied Ms. Hitchcock, the play's director and a teacher at Fleischman. She sat watching her students rehearse.

"Pssst! Over here!" Keisha looked onstage. A head and arm poked out from behind the oversized red velvet curtain. It was Alyssa. She waved them over to the stage.

Keisha snatched up the pile of costumes, and she and Carlos made their way down the aisle. They climbed a set of side steps to head backstage. Carlos moved awkwardly, trying not to drop his stack of boxes again.

A podium was set up just inside the curtain. Next to the podium was a row of thick ropes that

stretched to the stage's rafters. As the stage manager, Alyssa wore a headset and carried a thick, three-ring binder. A necklace with a single key on the end hung around her neck. She hovered near the podium, using a small flashlight to study her script and tell the other actors when to be on stage.

While Frankie basked solo in the limelight, the play's stage crew hustled about backstage. The black-clothed kids were sliding sets into place and preparing props on a nearby table.

All except one.

Jaden stood near the prop table, transfixed by Frankie. The sixth grader had signed up for the drama club mostly because Frankie was a part of it. His wide eyes stared out at her, and he hung on her every word like a lovelorn puppy.

"Hang the costumes and set the boxes here for now, please," Alyssa whispered, pointing to a metal clothing rack set up by the prop table.

As Keisha and Carlos unloaded their costumes, the magical onstage spell broke and

Jaden turned his attention from Frankie to his friends. "Oh, hey guys," he said dreamily.

"'Sup, Jaden?" Carlos asked.

"Just taking a break from moving sets." Jaden shook his head and pointed to the stage. "Boy, she's awesome, isn't she?" he asked.

"Yeah," Keisha grumbled. "She's something, all right."

"Thanks for helping out," Alyssa said, sighing as she moved to the prop table alongside them. "We're running short on stagehands, and opening night is just a week away."

"What do you mean? What happened to the stagehands?" Keisha asked.

"The ghost," Jaden whispered.

"Ghost? What ghost?" Carlos asked.

Alyssa nodded. She clutched her thick binder across her chest. "We've all heard it," she said. "Unexplained noises. Scratches, screeches, and other weird sounds."

"Are you sure it's not just the school's air-conditioning or something making noises?"

Carlos asked skeptically. "Or someone playing a prank?"

Alyssa shook her head. "I've heard it. It's a high-pitched screeching that echoes through the whole theater. It's scared so many kids, they've backed out on us."

"We've barely got enough crew members to go on," Jaden added.

"And you haven't been frightened away yet, Mr. Scaredy Pants?" Keisha joked. "Wow. I guess your love for Frankie is stronger than I thought."

"My what?" Jaden blushed. His cheeks burned so red Keisha could see them even in the dusky backstage shadows. "I don't . . . that's . . . heh." He took off his baseball cap and scratched his head nervously.

Alyssa checked the stage, and then removed her necklace. "I'll be right back," she said to Keisha and her friends. "I'm going to wheel the costume rack over to the dressing room while I have a chance." She held up the key. "Ms. Hitchcock gave me one of the school's skeleton

keys. It opens any door. I don't trust anyone else with it." She quickly pushed the metal rack filled with costumes further backstage, disappearing behind the set pieces.

"You know," Carlos said, "Snoops, Inc., could look into this whole so-called 'ghost' thing. Whaddaya think?" He had that twinkle in his eyes, the kind that usually led to the group solving a mystery. Or getting into trouble, though the two things usually went hand in hand.

"We could?" Jaden asked, gulping hard.

"Well, sure," Carlos said. "I mean, it's not like ghosts are real, Jaden. There's obviously a simple explanation for the noises. Plus, it's not like anything else strange is happening around here, right?"

And then, as if on cue, the theater was plunged into total darkness.

CHAPTER 3

LIGHTS OUT!

On stage, Frankie let out a frightened scream.

"Frankie!" Jaden yelled. He stumbled forward, only to trip on the prop table, loudly knocking some of the props to the floor. "Ow!" he said with a hiss of pain. "That was a bad idea."

Keisha could barely see her nose in front of her face. As her eyes adjusted to the darkness, she noticed a flashlight beam heading toward them.

"What's going on?" It was Alyssa. The beam from her tiny flashlight was joined by the blue glow of Carlos' cell phone. Around them, crew members' feet shuffled. Voices whispered.

"Everyone stay calm!" Ms. Hitchcock's nasally voice carried through the auditorium. "Frankie, my dear, are you all right?"

"No!" Frankie shouted. "I can't see a thing!"

"But are you hurt?"

"Uh, yeah," she snipped back. "Emotionally. I was just in the middle of my biggest monologue of the whole show."

"Kevin, what's going on?" Alyssa spoke into her headset. "Did you or Hayden do that?"

Faintly, Keisha could hear someone in the headset shout, "No!"

"Come on," Carlos said to a couple of kids nearby. He waved his light at them. "Follow me."

Slowly but surely, the kids behind the set bumbled their way out onto the stage. Alyssa and Carlos led them with their lights, until the entire group was huddled on stage. It wasn't entirely

dark. Other than the glow of phones and tablets, Keisha spied a sliver of light cutting through the auditorium from one of the half-open back doors. Alyssa hurried backstage with her flashlight to make sure everyone was safe.

"Kevin, can you or Hayden get the lights back on?" Ms. Hitchcock asked into her own headset. She stood at the base of the stage, looking back to the rear of the auditorium. A cluttered control room with a glass window was set into the back wall. The control room was where they ran the spotlights and stage lights for the theater production. Hayden was working in the booth with a boy named Kevin Deutch. Twin flashlight beams danced in the booth.

"It's the ghost," one of the boys in the group huddled on stage whispered.

"Don't say that," a girl replied, her voice trembling.

"The theater is haunted," the boy said.

"I am seriously creeped out right now," another girl added.

Suddenly the lights flickered, dimmed, and then surged on to full. Keisha squinted against the harsh light. Many kids shielded their eyes with their hands. Carlos immediately searched around the stage, as if looking for clues.

"Nice work, Kevin," Ms. Hitchcock said into her headset.

Kevin was a lanky boy with a sprout of curly hair atop his head. He stood in front of the glass booth window next to Hayden. They were both shrugging. "It wasn't us," Keisha heard Kevin respond over the headset.

Jaden adjusted his hat and approached Frankie. "Are you all right?" he asked her.

"Ugh. Fine," she said, brushing him off like a speck of dust. Then she hopped off the stage, walked past Ms. Hitchcock, and declared, "I'm taking a break."

"Good idea," Ms. Hitchcock said, ignoring Frankie's rudeness. "In fact, why don't we all call it a day. We can return tomorrow for another rehearsal. After we check the lights and make

sure everything's working, of course. Opening
night is right around the corner."

Keisha looked over and saw Alyssa staring
with a sour expression at Frankie as she breezed
out of the auditorium. "Everything okay?"
Keisha asked.

Alyssa shrugged, slipping off her headset.
"It's just Frankie," she said. "Acting like the
world revolves around her. She turned into a real
diva after getting cast as the lead."

"After?" Keisha had to disagree with that one.

"I'd be able to deal with it if she was able to
hit her mark once in a while."

"Mark? What's that?" Keisha asked.

"The little pieces of tape on the stage," Alyssa
explained. "They tell a performer where they
need to stand for the spotlight to hit them. Like
the one right there."

She pointed to a small X made out of orange
tape, near the outline of what looked like a door
in the stage floor.

As they spoke, a girl with vibrant green eyes approached. She held a play script in her hand. "Alyssa? Can I speak to you?" the girl asked quietly.

"Sure thing, Olive." The girl walked backstage, and Alyssa turned to Keisha again. "Olive Robbins is Frankie's understudy. If Frankie gets sick or something, Olive would fill in for her," she explained.

"Olive studies hard and knows her stuff," Alyssa continued. "My job would be much easier if she were in the lead role, that's for sure."

Alyssa followed Olive while Keisha, Carlos, and Jaden remained on the stage. Keisha spied Hayden in the sound booth with Kevin, wrapping up and shutting down the equipment.

"You know," Carlos said, "ghost rumors aside, I get the feeling something funny is going on around here."

Keisha placed her hands on her hips. "I was thinking the exact same thing."

CHAPTER 4

SPOOKED

"Dude, ghosts don't exist."

Carlos was seated in the overstuffed, torn chair at Snoops HQ. His feet were propped up on the wooden desk. Jaden sat across from him in another old chair. An issue of *Ghost Pirates* lay open on his lap.

The four young sleuths all lived together in
the same apartment building. They had made
their office in one of the storage units in the
basement. The walls were made of chain link
fence, and the door was a small gate with
a padlock.

Unlike the other storage units, their space
was not filled with boxes of holiday decorations,
old clothes, or creepy old ventriloquist dummies,
like those owned by Mr. Heckles on the second
floor. The Snoops space had just a simple desk, a
couple of chairs, a lamp, and an old file cabinet.

"They do exist," Jaden countered. "Haven't
you watched the show *Ghost Grabbers*? They
check out haunted houses and record ghosts
and stuff."

"I don't buy it," Carlos said.

"It's not impossible, though," Hayden added.
She sat cross-legged on the floor. Snuggled in
her lap was Agatha, the stray orange tabby cat
who hung around the Snoops office. She was
their unofficial team mascot.

A grape sucker was wedged against the right side of Hayden's mouth. "One of my friends in the Young Forensics Club, Mona, is part of a paranormal group. She told me once that about half the people in the United States believe in ghosts."

"Do you?" Carlos asked.

"I haven't seen one," she said. "But that doesn't mean they don't exist."

Keisha, who was leaning against the file cabinet, joined in on the conversation. "Hayden, you were in the control booth with Kevin when the lights went out. Is it possible he just flipped a switch and lied about not knowing what happened to cover his mistake?"

Hayden shook her head. "No, Kevin's a type-A personality. He's very organized and keeps everything in its proper place. He wouldn't have done that."

"I noticed that the light was still on in the hall outside the auditorium," Keisha recalled. "The rest of the school didn't seem to be affected by the blackout. Just the theater."

"So maybe someone tripped the circuit breaker," Carlos suggested.

"But why?" asked Keisha.

Carlos shrugged. "Maybe it's the same joker pretending to be a ghost."

"Or someone who really doesn't want the drama club to perform the play," Hayden suggested.

"Why would someone want to stop the play?" Jaden asked.

"Dunno," Carlos said. "But we're gonna find out."

* * *

"Well, I don't think it was the circuit breaker," Keisha said.

She and Carlos stood in the school hallway the following day after class, staring at a door marked Electrical. The thick door was shut tightly.

"Unless the door was unlocked yesterday, nobody would have gotten in there," Keisha said, trying to turn the door handle. It wouldn't budge.

"Unless they had a key," Carlos said. "Like maybe a skeleton key from Ms. Hitchcock."

Keisha laughed. "Are you saying you think Alyssa killed the stage lights yesterday? She was taking the costumes to the dressing room."

"Maybe she took a detour."

Keisha shook her head. "I know Alyssa," she said. "No way it's her."

"Let's poke around at play practice," Carlos said. "See what's what."

Ms. Hitchcock hadn't arrived, so play practice hadn't started yet. Several crew members, including Alyssa, huddled together going over items in the stage manager's thick binder. They all wore black shirts and jeans. The actors were in full costume, wearing many of the dresses and cowboy hats Keisha and Carlos had delivered the day before. It was funny to see cowboys reading lines together. Keisha spied Hayden and Kevin standing near the control room.

Frankie Dixon was center stage. Naturally. She looked the part of a woman from the Old West.

Her costume was a pink, frilly, long-sleeved dress with a white bonnet. Keisha found it strange seeing Frankie not wearing her usual trendy clothes and jewelry. The actress was rehearsing from her script, each gesture a grand movement.

Keisha and Carlos had barely entered the auditorium when Frankie stopped, swiveled, and turned back. "Did you hear that?"

"Hear what?" someone asked.

"It's the ghost," Frankie said. "It's back!"

Keisha beelined for the stage. A few other kids whispered and directed their attention to Frankie. Sure enough, as she bounded up the stairs at the side of the stage, Keisha heard a metallic clinking sound. It sounded like ghostly chains rattling and seemed to come from everywhere and nowhere all at once.

"Everyone be quiet," Carlos directed the kids. He was right at Keisha's heels. Together, they made their way backstage.

Even with the curtains pulled open, the backstage area was cloaked in shadows. Keisha

could see the large set pieces made to look like Old West buildings. Carlos had his phone out and was using the flashlight app to see again, like he had the day before.

"It's the ghost, isn't it?" Frankie hissed from behind her. Keisha jumped. The two girls had barely spoken to each other since The Fallout, so she was kind of surprised to hear Frankie talking to her.

Only, she wasn't. She was talking to Jaden. He stood near Frankie, trying his best to be brave. "I'll keep you safe," he said, his voice quavering.

"Oh, brother," Keisha whispered.

A series of scrapes and screeches suddenly erupted backstage. "There!" Carlos tried to follow the sound. But he stopped, unsure which direction to turn. In the midst of the ghostly noises, Keisha heard another sound — the soft tinkling of metal. The metallic jangle was coming from her right.

"Carlos, wait a second," she said. As she spoke, the tinkling sound sped up, followed by a

loud thunk and a crack. Keisha looked up to see large objects moving in front of her. It took her a second to figure out what was happening. When she did, her heart began to race.

"The sets!" she shouted. "WATCH OUT! They're falling!"

CHAPTER 5

THE PLOT THICKENS

Like a group of large dominoes, the flats that made up the Western town began to topple over. *Crash!* One of the flats knocked over some stage lights sitting nearby.

Keisha stepped back, pulling Carlos by the arm. They raced out of the backstage area just as the sets crashed to the stage floor in a cloud of dust.

Boom! The stage shook as a large, heavy light fell at one end near Frankie. The play's star let out a blood-piercing scream as it punched a hole in the stage floor. As the dust cleared, a wooden wagon wheel, part of a prop stagecoach, rolled across the stage and wobbled over.

"That was close! Thanks," said Carlos.

"No problem," Keisha said. Her attention wasn't on her friends, though. It was still on the backstage area, where she'd heard the jingling sound.

"Are you okay?" Jaden asked Frankie. He was helping her off the floor, where she had landed next to the hole in the stage floor.

"I'm terrified," Frankie said. "Thank goodness you're here."

"Just doing what I can," Jaden said.

"My hero." Frankie gave him a squeeze, and Jaden's cheeks flushed.

Keisha rolled her eyes. The two hadn't been as close to the falling sets and lights as she and

Carlos had been. But no one was checking to see if *they* were all right.

She began to walk backstage again, waving to Carlos as she did. "Follow me," she said. She snatched the phone from his hand and led with the flashlight.

"What is it?" Carlos asked.

"I heard a sound, right before the sets and lights fell," she explained. "I think someone was back here, and pushed the sets over on purpose." She stepped over one of the flats and then slipped behind another toward the back corner of the theater. They passed a row of ropes weighed down by sandbags and a stack of tables and chairs. Keisha stumbled over the edge of a large, dark rug, and came to a stop right where she'd heard the noise.

But the space was empty.

"It's just . . . a dead end," Carlos said.

And it was. The two back walls of the theater, painted black, were all they saw. No door. No window. No escape. If someone had

knocked over the sets and lights, they'd either escaped in the ruckus — or hadn't been there in the first place.

* * *

Ms. Hitchcock gasped when she saw the destruction onstage. "Oh no! I'm so thankful no one was hurt."

"Hurt? We could have been killed!" Frankie said dramatically.

The theater kids were standing together at the base of the stage. Some sat in the faded red auditorium seats, including Frankie's understudy, Olive Robbins.

"I'll have to cancel today's practice, as well," Ms. Hitchcock said. "And until we find out what's causing all of this, I think we'll have to hold off on any further practices, at least for now."

"Wait . . . are we canceling the play?" Kevin asked.

Ms. Hitchcock mulled it over. "I'll have to speak with Principal Snider, but until I can be sure that

whatever nonsense is going on is cleared up . . . I'm afraid, at the very least, it'll have to be postponed."

The news sent the drama club into an uproar. Several of the kids began to plead with Ms. Hitchcock to change her mind. Others once again blamed the ghost for cursing their production. "Flickering lights, strange noises, and now falling sets?" Kevin said. "It's just not . . . logical."

The Snoops found a quiet spot near the back of the auditorium to talk.

"So what now?" Keisha asked.

Carlos chewed on his bottom lip a minute. "Well, if we think someone is trying to sabotage the production —"

"You mean a ghost?" Jaden interrupted.

"Dude," Carlos said, "I don't know how many times I have to tell you . . ."

"But . . . what if it *is* a ghost?" Hayden said.

Keisha couldn't believe it. Hayden, the smartest and most logical of the group, was agreeing with her brother? Hayden continued. "Keisha, you said yourself, the area backstage was a dead end.

Nobody was hiding back there. What if there really is an angry spirit trying to curse the play?"

Keisha shook her head. "There has to be an easy explanation. And I can't believe I'm saying this, but I think they're targeting Frankie. She's the star of the play, and for sure the least-loved cast member. The lights went out when she was giving her monologue on stage. Then the sets and lights came crashing down when she was the only cast member rehearsing nearby."

"It makes sense," Carlos said. "Way more than Casper the Not-So-Friendly Ghost trying to scare us."

"So do we have any suspects then?" Hayden asked. "I mean, aside from almost everyone here, including us?" She gave her brother a playful shove. "Well, maybe not this guy."

Keisha looked out at the seats and saw Alyssa and Olive talking quietly to one another. She thought back to their conversation the day before, when Alyssa griped to her about Frankie and how the play would be much better without her

in the lead. Then Keisha thought of the skeleton key that Alyssa had used before. She didn't think her friend was capable of sabotaging the play because of a grudge. But often, the most logical answer is the right one.

"I hate to say it," Keisha said. "But yeah. Carlos and I have a suspect in mind."

CHAPTER 6

PIZZA AND A SURPRISE GUEST

"That's crazy," Hayden said when Keisha had shared her suspicions. "Alyssa's, like, the hardest-working person here. No way she'd want to ruin everything over a stupid grudge."

"It's the only lead we have," Carlos said. "So for now, as nuts as it sounds, we're gonna have to run with it."

"Well, if she is sabotaging the stage, it's worked," Hayden said. She pointed at the cluster of kids starting to file out of the theater. Alyssa turned back, saw the junior sleuths still standing in the back, and walked over to join them.

"Some of us are heading over to Zippy 'Za for some pizza," she said. "We're gonna try to drown our sorrows in pepperoni and extra cheese. Want to join us?"

Keisha nodded. "Yeah," she said. "Sounds cool." Plus, it was a good chance to chat with their number-one suspect.

Hayden and Jaden passed, saying they had to head home for dinner with their parents. "Plus," Hayden added cryptically, "I have to chat with one of my YFC friends about something."

"Count me in," Carlos said. "I can't pass up Zippy 'Za. Besides, my dad has to work late at the store tonight. It'll be good to hang out for awhile."

Carlos' dad owned Diaz Groceries, across the street from their apartment building. Keisha envied Carlos and how his dad worked so close to

home. Her mom worked long hours across the city as a bank teller. Her dad drove a garbage truck for the city. He was usually already at work when she woke up in the morning for school.

Zippy 'Za wasn't too far from Fleischman Middle School. It was still light out, and the busy streets were alive with the sound of rumbling trucks and honking horns. Carlos and Keisha walked toward the back of the crowd of drama kids as they made their way down the sidewalk.

When they arrived at the small pizza place it was fairly full, but the kids found a long table in the back near a row of old arcade games. The pizza joint's owners grew up in the 1980s. Catchy pop songs floated through the air. Most of the arcade games were the same ones the kids' parents had played when they were in middle school. One game had a round yellow creature that was chased by colorful ghosts around a maze. In another game, a plumber tried to jump over barrels thrown at him by a large monkey.

They ordered pizza, and Keisha was just starting to bite into her gooey slice of Veggie Extreme when the door of Zippy 'Za opened.

"Well, that's unexpected," Carlos said as Frankie Dixon walked through the door.

Frankie was the last person Keisha expected to see. In fact, she was the last person all of them expected to see.

"Hey, Frankie," Carlos said in his usual charming way.

Frankie's lip twitched, like it wanted to smile but was afraid to do it. "So this is where you guys hang out, huh?" she asked.

"Yeah," Alyssa said. She was seated next to Keisha. "Want a slice?"

"Okay." Frankie found an open chair next to Kevin and sat down. Everyone around her held their breath, like they were waiting for a bomb to go off. Frankie's nose wrinkled as she took a plate from a stack in the middle of the table. "Charming place," she said sarcastically.

As Frankie began to silently eat, the drama club returned to its usual chattering self. Keisha couldn't help staring at her old friend, watching as Frankie just ate her pizza and checked her phone.

Keisha had known Frankie for years, and she could tell when Frankie was scared. She must have been frightened by her close call at the theater and wanted to be around others. She was just too stubborn to admit it.

"You two used to be friends, didn't you?"

The voice took Keisha by surprise. Olive Robbins was sitting beside her now. The meek understudy was watching Frankie as well, peeling the label from her water bottle.

"Yup," Keisha replied.

"And here I thought being her understudy was hard." Olive snickered at her own joke. "What happened?"

"I don't like to talk about it," Keisha said. "Let's just say she wasn't always so . . . Frankie . . . about everything."

"You mean she didn't always buy roles away from people who really wanted them?"

Keisha turned to Olive. The girl's head was down, focusing on her water bottle label. "What do you mean?" Keisha asked.

"All the new costumes, the new display case," Olive said. "Her dad's helping out a lot. Seems like the least Ms. Hitchcock could do is give Frankie a part." She shrugged. "It just happened to be mine."

Keisha looked at Olive in a new light. Though the girl was thin and shy, there was an edge in her voice when she spoke about Frankie.

Suddenly a second name had been added to their suspect list.

Two loud horn honks blasted from outside the pizzeria. Frankie slid the plate away from her and quickly stood. "Ugh. So dirty," she said. "Well, that's Daddy. It's been a — well, I hate to use the word 'pleasure.' It's been . . . real."

Frankie wove her way around the tables toward the door. To get there, she had to pass

Keisha. As she came close to her old friend, Frankie stopped.

"Keisha," Frankie said quietly, "thanks for warning me about the sets today." The way she spoke, it seemed to Keisha like the apology burned coming out of her throat.

"No problem," Keisha said.

And that was it. Frankie ducked out of Zippy 'Za, on her way to better things. The drama kids didn't even watch her leave. Keisha glanced over to the arcade games and saw Alyssa and Olive standing and talking together.

Keisha hated to admit it, but a part of her actually felt sad for Frankie.

A small part. Like, a really tiny part.

But still . . .

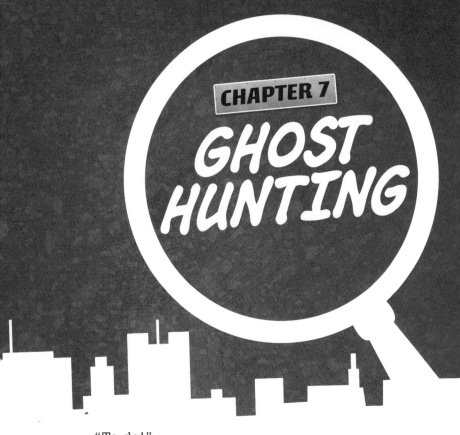

CHAPTER 7

GHOST HUNTING

"Ta-da!"

Hayden held her arms out in front of her. Sitting on the desktop were three identical devices. They looked to Keisha like they had come from a science-fiction movie.

"What are they?" she asked.

"They're going to help us prove once and for all if there's a ghost in the Fleischman auditorium," Hayden replied.

It was the evening after the gathering at
Zippy 'Za, and the Snoops crew was meeting
in their office. Keisha had just finished eating
dinner with her parents. Her father had taken up
his usual spot, seated in his recliner watching
baseball. Her mom was preparing to go to the
Parent-Teacher Association meeting at school.

Hayden picked up one of the devices. "I
contacted Mona, my YFC friend," she explained.
"You know, the one in the paranormal group.
She's local, so she loaned us some of her
equipment."

"Wait, so do we get to be like the *Ghost
Grabbers* now?" Jaden asked.

"Sure do," Hayden said. She scratched Agatha
behind one ear. The cat lifted its head, purring,
not a care in the world.

"What's this thing?" Keisha asked as Hayden
passed it over to her. She gripped its handle as
she studied the device. A row of lights — green,
yellow, and red — flickered as she moved the
contraption back and forth.

"It's an electromagnetic field detector," Hayden said. "An EMF meter. It reads the magnetic currents in the air. Any changes in the current — such as from a ghost — will make the light go from green to red."

"This is crazy." Keisha wielded the meter, aiming it around the office. The green light turned solid and remained there.

Two other similar devices were on the desk, along with a fourth. The last one was silver and looked like a thin, old camera. Hayden plucked it off the desk. "This is an EVP recorder. EVP stands for Electronic Voice Phenomena. It records faint sounds, so we can hear if a spirit is trying to contact us."

Jaden shuddered. "Are we seriously gonna do this?" he asked.

"If this is what it takes to prove this whole ghost rumor is nonsense," Carlos said, "then I'm in."

"The PTA meeting starts at the school in a half hour," Keisha said. "It's the perfect chance

to sneak into the auditorium while everyone is preoccupied."

Hayden began to fill her backpack with the ghost-hunting equipment.

"All right, Snoops," Carlos said. "Let's do this."

* * *

The front door of Fleischman was propped open. A sign reading "PTA Meeting in Cafeteria" was taped to it. Keisha and her mom walked together up the stone steps, the rest of the Snoops right behind. Principal Snider, an imposing man with a barrel chest and a bald head, stood just inside the door. He greeted parents as they arrived.

"Ah, Mrs. Turner," he said. "A pleasure to see you."

"Likewise," Keisha's mom replied.

"And if it isn't Fleischman's very own crime solvers." Principal Snider and Snoops, Incorporated, were on good terms. Most of the time, anyway. "When Ms. Hitchcock informed me

about postponing the production, I wasn't surprised to discover the four of you were involved."

"We just want to help the school, sir," Carlos said with a smile.

"Yes, well, for the sake of the drama club's hard work, I hope you can." He nodded toward the hallway on his left. "The school's gymnasium is open to students who've tagged along with their parents," he explained. "Go shoot some hoops or toss a football. Better yet, maybe work on finishing your homework."

"Sure thing, Principal Snider," Carlos said.

The four friends split from Keisha's mom, who headed toward the cafeteria. As they walked down the hall toward the gym, Keisha looked back over her shoulder. Principal Snider was greeting another parent who'd just walked in. "We're clear," she said.

The foursome took a sharp turn, away from the gym and down a darkened side hall. They made their way quickly and quietly toward the auditorium.

"Man, this place is weird at night," Jaden said. "It's so quiet."

Keisha felt it too. Without the constant hum of activity and buzz of fluorescent lights, Fleischman felt even more like the kind of place that could be haunted.

The door to the auditorium was cracked open. Keisha led the way inside the pitch-black theater, leaving the door the way she found it after all four team members were inside.

"Where's the light switch?" Jaden whispered. "I can't see anything."

"No lights," Hayden whispered. "Flashlights only."

A beam of light suddenly shone in front of Keisha, hitting Jaden right in the eyes. "Ah!" he hollered out. "Watch it!"

"Sorry," Carlos said.

They huddled together, walking as one down the nearest aisle toward the stage. Carlos swung his flashlight back and forth, illuminating the old seats and sending shadows into a frenzied dance.

Keisha could hear Jaden's shaky breathing. She held on to Hayden's trembling hand. Keisha hated being scared, but she had to admit, this was kind of creepy.

"Okay," Hayden said when they'd reached the bottom of the stage. She rummaged in her

backpack, pulled out the EMF meters, and handed them to the others. She kept the audio recorder for herself. Green lights glowed in the dark from each of the meters.

"Nothing yet," Carlos said.

"Give it a minute," Hayden said.

"What if we only make the ghost angrier?" Jaden asked. "It already tried to knock a bunch of buildings onto Carlos just because he was looking for it."

"Shhh!" Hayden said quietly. "Mona said we need to stay as quiet as possible."

Keisha stared at the green light and tried to remain still. The others did the same.

Suddenly a low growl rumbled like thunder through the silence. "What was that?!" Hayden gasped, checking her audio recorder. "Was it the ghost?!"

"Sorry," Jaden said. "My bad. That was my stomach. I'm, uh, kind of hungry again."

Hayden rolled her eyes. "Unbelievable," she murmured.

They resumed their silence, standing like statues. A few moments passed. Then Keisha heard a thin screech from somewhere on stage.

"Not my stomach," Jaden proclaimed. "Totally not my stomach."

"The ghost," Hayden whispered.

Goosebumps crawled up Keisha's spine and along her arms. Though the lights on their meters were still bright green, the sound on stage continued. A rattle and scuff joined the scrape.

Carlos quietly climbed the stage steps. The fallen set pieces had been stacked along the far wall, well out of the way. Keisha was a few paces behind Carlos, trying to stay close. She was trying even harder not to admit that she was actually, genuinely terrified.

The scraping, haunting sounds grew louder as they crossed the stage. The Snoops' flashlight beams swung left and right.

"Where is it?" Jaden whispered, prompting a slug to the arm from his sister. She pressed her finger to her lips.

Keisha tried to keep the flashlight in her hand from shaking. Carlos was near the theater's back wall, the sound louder than ever.

Keisha glanced at her meter. The light was . . .

"Green?" she whispered. "But that means there's no —"

"Ghost!" Jaden screamed.

He pointed to a large pair of glowing eyes that had suddenly appeared right in front of them!

CHAPTER 8

SUSPICIOUS BEHAVIOR

"AHHHHH!"

The Snoops screamed in unison and fell backward like a set of bowling pins being knocked over. Jaden fell first, his flashlight striking the stage floor and going dark. Hayden was next. Her light landed on the floor and spun wildly in circles. Keisha and Carlos stumbled but stayed on their feet — barely.

The shadowy spirit with glowing eyes stared up at them, waiting for them to move.

"It's the ghost!" Jaden hollered.

"No," Carlos said, shining his light on the critter. "It's not a ghost. It's a raccoon."

Sure enough, the frightening beast before them was nothing more than a fluffy, scared raccoon. It blinked and shied away from the light.

"Like, a ghost raccoon?" Jaden pointed his EMF meter at it.

"Just a regular raccoon, dude," Keisha said.

The raccoon growled at them before quickly spinning around. Its claws scraped the wooden floor as it dashed away. Carlos trailed the raccoon with his flashlight, and the Snoops watched it scurry under a ventilation cover in the wooden stage. The terrifying screeching sounds they'd heard before returned as the raccoon raced along inside the ventilation shaft under the floor.

"The ghost sounds we heard are just the raccoon in the ventilation shaft," Carlos explained. "It must have built a home under the stage."

"So there isn't a ghost?" Jaden asked.

"No ghost," Carlos said. "I don't want to say 'told you so,' but —"

"Don't say it," Hayden said.

Keisha clicked off her EMF meter. The green light faded out. "Okay," she said, "that explains the noises. But what about the falling sets and lights? And what about the blackout? No way a raccoon can do that. Someone's still involved."

"We should hightail it out of here before we get busted," Carlos said.

The Snoops stowed their gear back in Hayden's pack. Keisha could tell Hayden was pretty bummed that there hadn't been a ghost in the theater.

"A raccoon," Jaden said as they all rushed up the aisle, back to the door. "Boy, wait until Ms. Hitchcock hears about this."

As they reached the auditorium door, Keisha came to a quick stop. "Hold up," she whispered, stretching out her arm.

No one spoke. Outside, in the hall, the sound of whistling drifted toward them.

"Kill the flashlights," Carlos said. They did, casting the theater into total darkness.

Keisha watched through the gap in the door as the whistling grew louder. Along with it came the squeaking sound of a stuck wheel and the jingling of metal.

Mr. Ron strolled along the hall, pushing his cleaning cart. The large ring of keys on his belt tinkled with each step. He did not seem to notice the cracked-open auditorium door. He stopped briefly, just out of sight, whistling the whole time. Then he continued down the hall.

The Snoops waited another minute. Then Keisha stuck her head out the door. The hall was empty. "The coast is clear," she whispered to the others.

The young sleuths slipped from the theater and hurried off to join the other kids in the gymnasium.

* * *

With the mystery of the supposed ghost solved, the Snoops set their minds back on the real mystery.

Who was sabotaging the production of the play? Was Alyssa trying to put a stop to the play for some reason? Or was Olive trying to scare Frankie away from the part that she wanted for herself?

The following morning at school, the Snoops crew prepared to head to their separate classes. Carlos said, "I walk by Ms. Hitchcock's room on my way to first period. I'll drop in and tell her about the raccoon."

"And I've got social studies with Alyssa first thing this morning," Keisha said. "She's still our main suspect. I'll keep an eye on her."

They split up and Keisha headed down the hall toward her locker. As she passed the auditorium, she heard a shrill voice cry out, "Who did this?!"

"Frankie?" Keisha turned back.

Frankie stood pointing at the display case. In black marker, someone had scribbled the word CANCELED across the glass. Alongside it, a flowing ghost with large black eyes had been drawn. The ghost was shouting, "BOO!"

No one seemed to care that Frankie was upset. One boy snickered as he walked by. Another made ghostly hooting sounds.

"This is unacceptable!" Frankie stomped her feet. "Daddy paid good money to fix up this dusty old display." Keisha felt a twinge of guilt. She really should go talk to Frankie and try to calm her down. Instead, her ex-BFF stormed off before Keisha could do a thing.

Keisha began to head off down the hall again. As she did, she spied Alyssa and Olive standing together. The two girls were pointing at the display case. She watched as the two girls moved off down the hall together.

"Wait a second," Keisha muttered. "Social studies is the other direction. Where are they going?"

Keisha hated being late to class. But there was still time before the bell rang. She followed Alyssa and Olive as they buzzed down the hall. Alyssa stopped in front of the door to the school's media

center. Keisha pulled up too, and took a sip from a water fountain, pretending not to notice the girls. In the metallic reflection from the fountain, she saw Alyssa and Olive duck into the media center.

Keisha followed.

At first, she thought she'd lost track of the other girls. Perhaps they'd sneaked out the door on the other side of the large room. Keisha hurriedly glanced one way, then the other. Then she caught a flash of color from Alyssa's shirt in the distance. The two girls were headed down a row of nonfiction titles.

Keisha took the row beside them, the media center's carpeted floor hiding her steps. She could hear Alyssa whispering as she snuck closer . . . and closer . . .

"Here it is," Olive said. "Are you sure this plan will work?"

"It will work," Alyssa said. "Once Ms. Hitchcock sees what we've been doing, she'll agree with us. I know it."

"If you say so." Olive sounded nervous.

Keisha couldn't believe her ears. With *us*? The two girls were working together? The next smart play would have been to immediately find Carlos and tell him what she had learned. But Keisha, bullheaded and unafraid, stormed into the next row of books to confront the two conspiring girls.

She rounded the corner and pointed at them. "A-ha!" she shouted, her voice carrying in the quiet media center. "Busted!"

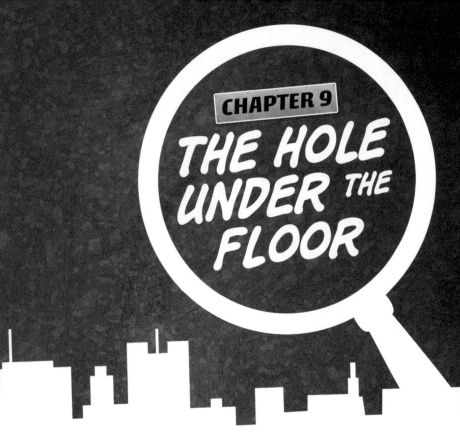

CHAPTER 9

THE HOLE UNDER THE FLOOR

"Keisha?" Alyssa was shocked to see her, Olive even more so. The sneaky understudy looked like a deer in headlights. She clutched a long, thin book to her chest.

"I can't believe it," Keisha said, shaking her head. "I mean, I know Frankie Dixon is a lot to handle and that she bought her way into a lead role. But trying to wreck the whole play just because of one person?"

Alyssa's face scrunched up. "Huh?"

Keisha wasn't buying it. "Don't give me that," she said. "I heard what you guys were just talking about. How sure you are that your plan will work? Alyssa, you're the only one with a key to the electrical room. You had plenty of time to push the sets over while Frankie was on stage and we were distracted by the silly raccoon."

"Raccoon?" Alyssa asked.

"Yeah, the so-called ghost? Turns out it was just a wild animal climbing in through the vents."

"So you think we're sabotaging the play?" Olive asked.

"Yeah," Keisha said. "Neither of you like Frankie Dixon, which is fair enough, I guess. But still . . ." She proudly placed her hands on her hips. "Your plan has officially crashed and burned. I can't'wait to tell Carlos."

Alyssa shook her head. "Keisha, I spent months on that play. Coming to school early, staying late. I would never do that to the rest of the cast and crew, regardless of how I feel about Frankie."

"Say what now?" It was Keisha's turn to be baffled.

"Olive, show her." Alyssa nodded, and Olive peeled the library book from her chest. She held it out to Keisha.

It was an old school yearbook, hard-covered, the edges frayed and bent. It was at least thirty years old. On the cover, kids with large, poufy hairdos waved and smiled.

"I don't understand," Keisha said.

"Here." Olive stepped over and took the yearbook from Keisha. She flipped it open until she found a page dedicated to the drama club. Hazy black-and-white photos showed a student production of a play. Kids wore space suits and bizarre, alien outfits. A cardboard moon hung from the rafters. A large spaceship made of wood and aluminum foil sat at center stage.

"Back in the day, the drama club was allowed to do whatever play they wanted," Alyssa said. "Students were even allowed to submit their own ideas and scripts for plays." She dug into her

backpack and came out with a stack of white paper held together with three fasteners.

"*Werewolves in Love*," Keisha read from the stack's top page. "By Alyssa Wentworth and Olive Robbins."

"We haven't told anybody," Alyssa said. "But yeah. We're gonna show our script and this yearbook to Ms. Hitchcock. Hopefully, she'll like our plan, and the next play the drama club performs will be ours."

Keisha was floored. She had no idea Alyssa liked to write. But it also put her back at square one. Both of the Snoops' suspects had been eliminated at the same time.

"So if you're not sabotaging the play," Keisha said. "And it isn't a ghost —" She held the yearbook open again, staring at the drama club photos.

And then she saw it.

A photo at the bottom of the page caught her eye. In it, the spaceman was standing in the middle of the stage. Smoke billowed around him as he descended into the stage floor.

The trap door in the stage, Keisha thought to herself. Then she remembered the fallen sets and the dead end behind them. Things were starting to look a little clearer.

"Hey, sorry I was being a jerk," she said. "I was way off."

"It's okay," said Alyssa. "This whole thing has everyone on edge. But promise to talk to me before pointing fingers next time?"

"You got it." Then Keisha had an idea. "Any chance we could check something out after school? I may need your key to the auditorium."

Alyssa shrugged. "No problem," she said. "Anything to help get the play back on track."

The first bell of the morning rang through the media center. Olive snatched the yearbook from Keisha's hand. "We've got to check this out and get to class," she said. She and Alyssa hustled off to the media specialist's desk.

"Meet you at the auditorium after school," Keisha called after them. Then she headed back into the bustling halls of Fleischman.

* * *

"A trapdoor." Carlos shook his head. "Of course."

The Snoops, along with Alyssa and Olive, huddled in a circle. They stared down at the stage floor, where a square hole yawned open before them.

Keisha had led the group backstage, to the dead-end corner where she'd tripped over the rug. She hadn't noticed it before. It was dark and, like it or not, she'd been thinking of ghosts at the time. But there in the floor was a trapdoor. It was similar to the one on the stage, which she'd

noticed in the yearbook photo. However, this one had been partially hidden by the rug.

"So . . ." Jaden looked down into the black hole. "Who's hopping in first?"

"I'll go." Keisha sat on the floor, dangling her feet over the edge. Carlos fired up his phone's flashlight app and shined the blue light into the hole. The drop wasn't far, maybe six feet at most.

Keisha slid down, landing solidly on the cement below.

"I'm okay." Keisha's words were nearly swallowed by the space around her. The beams above lightly scraped her head when she stood up straight. So she bent lower and crept forward. A thunk from behind her made her heart skip a beat, but it was just Carlos.

"Coast is clear," he said to the twins. "Come on down."

"Uh . . . I'm good!" Jaden replied nervously. "Thanks for the offer, though!"

Carlos' blue light filled the space. "Light switch," he said, finding it on the wall.

Keisha flicked it on.

A row of small bulbs sparked to life. They were strung like Christmas lights along one wall. Their light was faint, but it was enough to see the storage space around them.

What was once an empty area used to hide the entrance and exit of actors on stage was now stacked high with boxes. Old props and sets also filled the space. Including, Keisha was almost certain, the spaceship from the yearbook she'd seen that morning.

She brushed away a cobweb and glanced at a metal shelf set up along one wall. "Look," she said, stepping closer.

Directly above the shelf was an old, broken grate to the ventilation shaft above. The top row of the shelf was filled with garbage — old food wrappers, spoiled fruit, torn paper, and bits of cloth.

"Looks like we found where our so-called ghost likes to hang out," Carlos said. The raccoon was nowhere in sight.

"So whoever pushed over the set pieces snuck down here after they did it," Keisha deduced. Nearby, the dusty floor was scuffed and scraped with footprints. "And there's the proof."

Carlos used his phone to snap photos of the dusty footprints. Next to them were two large boxes. The top box was open. "These look pretty new, compared to the rest," Carlos said.

Keisha peered into the top box. It was filled with rolled-up posters, trophies, and photos. "Wait a minute . . ." She dug through the box, pulling out various items.

A photo caught her eye. It was a close-up of a smiling middle school student wearing an astronaut's jumpsuit. On the bottom of the photo were the words: *The Spaceman Cometh*, along with the actor's name.

All of the clues they'd found suddenly clicked into place. Keisha smiled. "I figured it out," she said. "I know who's behind the whole thing."

CHAPTER 10

A GRAND PERFORMANCE

"Are you sure you know what you're doing?" Frankie Dixon hugged her arms tightly across her chest. "The last time I was on this stage, I nearly became a Frankie pancake."

Keisha climbed the steps to the darkened stage. "What's wrong, Frankie?" Keisha asked sarcastically. "Don't you trust me?"

"I used to," Frankie muttered.

Keisha let the comment slide.

They moved to center stage. Keisha toed the tape X on the floor. "Should be any minute," she said.

The two girls stood awkwardly in the silence of the theater. They had spoken more to each other over the last few days than they had since The Fallout. Keisha wasn't about to admit that they could somehow mend their torn friendship, but . . .

Maybe they just needed time.

The auditorium door slammed closed. Frankie leaped back, clutching Keisha's arm tightly.

"I got your note," a voice called from the back of the theater. "Said you wanted to talk about *The Spaceman Cometh?*"

In the shadows, Keisha watched the newcomer stroll down the aisle toward them. With each step came the jingle of metal on metal, the same sound Keisha heard before the sets fell over.

"We know you knocked down the sets and stage lights," Keisha said. Her heart was thundering in her chest. Any harder and she might crack a rib. "And then you hid under the stage

while we all argued about the play being cursed by a ghost. Which is just a raccoon, by the way."

The newcomer laughed. "Ha! It's funny you mention that. I've been trying to shoo that pesky raccoon away for weeks now. Goofy thing won't leave. I was gonna call Animal Control, but then all those silly ghost rumors started up. It was doing a good job of scaring you kids, so I left it alone."

The newcomer reached the steps and climbed up. Keisha backed up as the shadow joined them on stage.

"So why'd you do it?" Keisha said.

The shadowy figure stopped and sighed. In the faint light, the girls could finally make out who it was.

"Mr. Ron?" Frankie blurted out.

"Yep," Keisha said. "We should have pieced it together earlier. We thought Alyssa used her key to get into the electrical room and kill the lights, but it was him. He knew about the storage space under the stage too." Keisha held up the photo she'd found in the box.

"Is that . . .?" Frankie asked.

"Little Ronald Harper, the 13-year-old creator of *The Spaceman Cometh.*"

The school janitor nodded. "Look, I never wanted to hurt anyone," he said. "And I'm sorry that stage light almost hit you, Frankie. I just . . . when I wrote and performed *The Spaceman Cometh*, it was the best feeling in the world. My photo was a permanent part of Fleischman history, on display for all to see." He pointed at Frankie. "And then she showed up and ruined everything."

"So you used the ghost angle to scare the drama club, hoping that Frankie would quit?" Keisha accused. "You even drew that ghost on the display case for added effect, didn't you?"

"Yeah," Mr. Ron said. "I'm not proud of it. But I walked past that display every day. Being in that play was the best moment of my life. Now, no one will remember me!"

Just then, a single spotlight cast a beam of light onto the stage. Mr. Ron held up an arm to shield his eyes from the brilliant light.

"Bravo! Nice work," came Carlos' voice. He and Jaden sat in the front row.

"Did you get all that, Hayden?" Keisha asked. She glanced back at the control room's window, where Hayden gave her a thumbs-up.

"Sorry, Mr. Ron," Keisha said.

"Ms. Hitchcock and Principal Snider are on their way," Carlos said.

The school janitor hung his head in shame. "I'm so sorry," he said.

Keisha couldn't help but feel sorry for him. All he'd wanted was to remain part of Fleischman's legacy. Now, he'd be remembered for all the wrong reasons.

* * *

Two nights later, the auditorium was filled with whistles and applause. It was the opening night of the play. Parents stood and cheered as the cast finished their first performance.

On stage, the cast jogged to the edge of the stage in small groups, clasped hands, and bowed.

The last curtain call was for Frankie Dixon. The applause swelled as she took a long, extravagant bow. Keisha even found herself clapping for her old friend.

Moments later, the cast and crew met the crowd in the halls outside the theater. Keisha wormed her way through with Carlos and Jaden close behind her.

"Hey, guys!" Hayden was waiting with Kevin Deutch and a few others next to the glass display case. The graffiti had been removed and Frankie's photo smiled out at them. But next to it, the old theater mementos had been returned. Young Ronald Harper, writer and star of *The Spaceman Cometh*, shared equal space with the star actress currently exiting the theater.

"Here she comes," Jaden said. He straightened his baseball cap and produced a large bouquet of flowers from behind his back. Frankie strolled toward the Snoops, not even glancing in their direction. She waved and said hello to the others in the crowd instead.

"Great job, Frankie." Jaden's voice cracked as he spoke and held out the flowers.

"Oh, aren't you just the sweetest." Frankie took the flowers and kissed Jaden on the cheek.

He looked like he was going to pass out. "I'm never gonna wash my face again," he whispered.

"Congrats, Frankie," Keisha said. For once, there wasn't an ounce of sarcasm in her words.

Frankie tilted her head up. She was about to speak when a shrill girl's voice shouted from behind Keisha, "Frankie! O-M-G! I love you!"

Frankie smiled and shouldered her way between Keisha and Carlos without saying a word. Keisha turned and saw her old friend being swarmed by spirit squad girls.

"Looks like the old Frankie is back," Carlos said.

"Are you upset?" Hayden asked Keisha.

Frankie looked back over her shoulder, briefly, a flash so quick Keisha barely caught it.

"Nah, not really," Keisha said. "Frankie can be a pain. But I think a lot of it is just an act."

THE END

Snoops, Inc. Case Report #002

Prepared by Keisha Turner

THE CASE:

Find out who wanted to stop the school's production of *Wagon's West!* Oh, and prove the school theater wasn't haunted. (Did I just write that?)

CRACKING THE CASE:

Carlos and I were just bringing costumes to the theater. But when the lights went out and Frankie (my ex-bestie) freaked out, the Snoops were on the case. Of course, the rumors about a ghost in the theater didn't help.

Ghosts aren't real. But to prove it we borrowed some EMF meters to investigate. EMF stands for Electromagnetic Field. EMF meters use electrical currents to detect charged objects. Electricians often use them to identify problems with wiring and power lines.

Paranormal experts say that an EMF meter can help detect the electrical residue left behind by a ghost. A lot of people believe in this stuff. But I don't buy it.

Anyway, the EMF meters helped us solve the so-called 'ghost' mystery. This led to finding out who wanted to shut down the play and Frankie's performance (although, it could have been anyone. She's not easy to get along with). So I guess the ghost gear really did help us . . .

CRACK THE CASE! ▃

WHAT DO YOU THINK?

1. Frankie isn't well liked by many members of the cast. Why is this? What examples from the story can you give to back up this opinion?

2. Have you ever been someplace that you thought was haunted? How did you feel while you were there? Did anything happen to make you think ghosts were nearby?

3. Explain in your own words why you think Mr. Ron sabotaged the play. Can you relate to how he felt? Could Mr. Ron have shared his feelings to the drama club in a better way?

WRITE YOUR OWN!

1. Keisha and Frankie were once best friends, but something happened that changed that. What do you think it was? Write a conversation between the two girls explaining their fight.

2. Think about a spooky place you know of that could be haunted. What do you think the ghost would be like? Write a description of the spirit and why it's haunting that location.

3. Pretend you are writing your own play for your school to perform. What would it be about? Write a summary describing the story and characters in your play.

GLOSSARY

CIRCUIT BREAKER (SUHR-kuht BRAKE-ur)—a switch that automatically stops the flow of electricity if the current becomes too strong

MONOLOGUE (MON-uh-log)—a long speech by one character in a drama

PARANORMAL (pair-uh-NOR-muhl)—having to do with an unexplained event that has no scientific explanation

PODIUM (POH-dee-uhm)—a stand with a slanted surface that holds a book or notes for someone who is speaking

SABOTAGE (SAB-uh-tahzh)—to damage, destroy, or interfere with something on purpose

SILHOUETTE (sil-oo-ET)—an outline of something that shows its shape

STAKEOUT (STAKE-out)—a situation in which someone watches a place to look for suspicious activity

VENTILATION SHAFT (ven-tuh-LAY-shuhn SHAFT)—part of a system that allows the flow of fresh air